How I Spent My Summer Vacation

written and illustrated by Mark Teague

Dragonfly Books ——— New York

For Rebecca and Jerry and Mark

Copyright © 1995 by Mark Teague

All rights reserved. Published in the United States by Dragonfly Books, an imprint of
Random House Children's Books, a division of Random House, Inc., New York.
Originally published in hardcover in the United States by Crown, an imprint of
Random House Children's Books, a division of Random House, Inc., New York, in 1995.

Dragonfly Books with the colophon is a registered trademark of Random House, Inc.

Visit us on the Web! www.randomhouse.com/kids

Educators and librarians, for a variety of teaching tools, visit us at
www.randomhouse.com/teachers

Library of Congress Cataloging-in-Publication Data
Teague, Mark.
How I spent my summer vacation / written and illustrated by Mark Teague.
p. cm.
Summary: A schoolboy tells his class about his summer vacation, during which
he joined a group of cowboys and stopped a cattle stampede.
ISBN 978-0-517-59998-3 (trade) — ISBN 978-0-517-59999-0 (lib. bdg.) — ISBN 978-0-517-88556-7 (pbk.)
[1. Cowboys—Fiction. 2. West (U.S.)—Fiction. 3. Stories in rhyme.] I. Title.
PZ8.3.T2184Ho 1995
[E]—dc20

MANUFACTURED IN CHINA

29 28 27

When summer began, I headed out west.

My parents had told me I needed a rest.

"Your imagination," they said, "is getting too wild.

It will do you some good to relax for a while."

So they put me aboard a westbound train

To visit Aunt Fern in her house on the plains.

But I was captured by cowboys,
A wild-looking crowd.
Their manners were rough
and their voices were loud.

"I'm trying to get to my aunt's house," I said.
But they carried me off to their cow camp instead.

The Cattle Boss growled, as he told me to sit,
"We need a new cowboy. Our old cowboy quit.
We could sure use your help. So what do you say?"
I thought for a minute, then I told him, "Okay."

Then I wrote to Aunt Fern, so she'd know where I'd gone.
I said not to worry, I wouldn't be long.

That night I was given a new set of clothes.

Soon I looked like a wrangler from my head to my toes.

But there's more to a cowboy than boots and a hat,

I found out the next day

And the day after that.

Each day I discovered some new cowboy tricks.

From roping

And riding

To making fire with sticks.

Slowly the word spread all over the land:
"That wrangler 'Kid Bleff' is a first-rate cowhand!"

The day finally came when the roundup was through.
Aunt Fern called: "Come on over. Bring your cowboys with you."

She was cooking a barbecue that very same day.
So we cleaned up (a little) and we headed her way.

The food was delicious. There was plenty to eat.
And the band that was playing just couldn't be beat.

But suddenly I noticed a terrible sight.
The cattle were stirring and stamping with fright.
It's a scene I'll remember till my very last day.
"They're gonna stampede!" I heard somebody say.

Just then they came charging. They charged right at *me!*
I looked for a hiding place—
a rock, or a tree.

What I found was a tablecloth spread out on the ground.

So I turned like a matador

And spun it around.

It was a new kind of cowboying, a fantastic display!

The cattle were frightened and stampeded . . . away!

Then the cowboys all cheered, "Bleff's a true buckaroo!"
They shook my hand and slapped my back,
And Aunt Fern hugged me, too.

And *that's* how I spent my summer vacation.

I can hardly wait for show-and-tell!